BIG APPLE BARN™

SADDLE UP, HAPPY!

WELCOME TO
BIG APPLE BARN!

BIG APPLE BARN™

SADDLE UP, HAPPY!

by **KRISTIN EARHART**

Illustrations by
JOHN STEVEN GURNEY

———

A
LITTLE APPLE
PAPERBACK

SCHOLASTIC INC.
New York Toronto London Auckland Sydney
Mexico City New Delhi Hong Kong Buenos Aires

To my sister Jill, who is always there when I need someone to talk to. Thanks for putting up with me . . . and my pony's green slime.
—K.J.E

ISBN-13: 978-0-439-90096-6
ISBN-10: 0-439-90096-4

Text copyright © 2007 by Kristin Earhart.
Illustrations copyright © 2007 by Scholastic Inc.
SCHOLASTIC, LITTLE APPLE, BIG APPLE BARN, and associated logos are trademarks and/or registered trademarks of Scholastic Inc.

12 11 10 9 8 7 6 5 4 3   7 8 9 10 11 12/0

Printed in the U.S.A.
First printing, March 2007

Contents

Chapter One

The Big News

Happy Go Lucky pricked his ears forward as Diane, his trainer, led him outside to the field. He could see that his friends were already there. He was in a hurry to join them, so he could get his fair share of sweet clover. The group of friends always ate at the same patch, and they always chatted as they munched on the tender clover buds.

But today something was different. Today Happy's friends weren't eating at all. They were only chatting! Big Ben, Goldilocks, and Sassafras were busy nodding as they took turns talking. Happy could hardly wait to hear what was so interesting.

Since he first came to Big Apple Barn at the beginning of the summer, Happy had always been turned out in the pasture with Goldi and Big Ben. Diane seemed to know that they all got along. It was true. Happy was glad to have the pretty caramel-colored pony and tall, noble show horse for friends. They had been at Big Apple Barn for years, and they gave him all kinds of good advice.

Sassy was new to the stables. She and Happy were both school ponies, and they looked out for each other. Sassy was an appaloosa. She was dark gray, except on her backside, which was white with black spots. Happy thought her coat matched her spunky personality.

But that wasn't what he was focusing on just then. He was wondering

what his friends were saying. Everyone looked so serious! Happy felt a little left out. Why hadn't they waited for him?

"Are you in a hurry, Happy?" Diane asked.

Happy realized that he had been walking fast and tugging at his lead line. It was something his mother, Gracie, had told him he should never do. It wasn't polite! Happy was glad his mother wasn't there to see his bad manners. But, in a way, he wished she were there. Happy had not seen his mother since he had come to Big Apple Barn. After he arrived, he learned that she had once lived there, too. She had been a school pony. In fact, Happy's mom and Goldi had been school ponies together. Happy liked his new life as a school pony, but he still missed his mom.

"Well, here you are, Happy," Diane said as she opened the pasture gate. She unhooked the lead line from Happy's halter and gave him a pat. "I hope that clover is as good as you're expecting."

Oh, I'm not after the clover today, Happy thought. *I want to know what's going on. I hope it's good news.* Happy walked into the pasture. As soon as Diane closed the gate, he bounded across the field at a bouncy canter.

"What are you talking about?" Happy asked as soon as he reached his friends.

"Well, it's very exciting," Big Ben answered. "But it isn't my news to share." Then he looked at Sassy. When his eyes met hers, Sassy quickly dropped her gaze to the ground.

If Happy didn't know better, he would think Sassy was being shy. But that wasn't like Sassy. She was usually brassy and bold.

"Do *you* have news, Sassy?" Happy questioned.

Sassy lifted her head and smiled at Happy. "I do," she said, looking proud. "I'm going to be in a show."

"A show?" Happy was surprised. He didn't know anyone who had been in a show other than Big Ben.

"Andrea is going to ride me," Sassy continued. Then she glanced at Happy and paused. "It's just a small show."

"But it's still exciting," Goldi said. "I remember my first show."

"Wait, you've been in a show, too?" Happy asked.

"Sure. I used to go to a lot of shows when I was younger. They were fun," Goldi explained.

"I think this show would be more fun if Happy could come as well," Sassy said.

Happy smiled at her. It was nice of Sassy to say so. She was a good friend. But that didn't change the facts. Sassy was going to the show, and Happy wasn't. He had not been invited.

Chapter Two

A Show Pony Returns

Happy didn't really want to go to the show, so it was easy for him to be excited for Sassy. A pony's first show was a big deal! Even though Sassy had been shy about it at first, it was clear that she was thrilled. The show was all she could talk about. Big Ben and Goldi eventually left to stand under the apple trees, but Sassy kept telling Happy all of the details.

"The show is at a place called Stillwater

Farms. Can you believe Andrea is going to be riding me?" Sassy asked. She tossed her mane, and Happy saw a sparkle in her eyes.

Andrea was Diane's older daughter. She had been around ponies her whole life, and she was a very good rider. Happy knew it was a compliment for Andrea to want to ride Sassy in a show.

But Happy wasn't jealous at all. He had enjoyed having Andrea for a rider when he first came to Big Apple Barn. But he liked Diane's younger daughter, Ivy, even better. Happy thought Ivy was the nicest person he knew. He had liked her even before she was his rider. Ivy was still a beginner, yet she knew just how to tell Happy to walk, trot, and canter. They also did some jumping — not as high as Happy could jump with other riders, but he didn't mind. He just liked being Ivy's lesson pony.

And he was happy to stick with lessons. Sassy, however, was ready to be a show pony.

"Do you think Andrea will braid my mane?" Sassy asked. "I hope so. I've always wanted my mane braided." Sassy wasn't even looking at Happy. She was staring off into the distance. "Maybe she'll do my tail, too. I've seen other ponies like that. Some even have their hooves glossed."

Happy was relieved when he saw Ivy at the pasture gate. He wasn't sure how much more show talk he could take!

"Time to come in Happy!" Ivy called.

"I gotta go," Happy said to Sassy. "Congratulations on the show."

"Oh, thank you," Sassy replied, sounding a little shy again.

Happy trotted to the gate and waited for Ivy to hook the lead line to his halter. He watched as Andrea strode into the pasture. He guessed she would bring Sassy inside. All the horses had to go back into the barn for dinner.

"So, did you hear that Andrea and Sassy are going to a show?" Ivy asked Happy before they had even left the field. "They are so lucky. I wish we could go."

Happy glanced over at Ivy. He was surprised that she wanted to go to the show, too. As much as Happy liked Ivy, he was glad they were not going to Stillwater Farms. Was that the only thing anyone could think about?

When he entered his stall and saw a gray

mouse in his feed bucket, Happy breathed a sigh of relief.

The mouse's name was Roscoe, and Happy knew him well. Roscoe had been Happy's first friend at Big Apple Barn. The young mouse was very clever, and he was a good listener. Happy felt like he could talk to Roscoe about anything.

"So I guess you've heard about Sassy," Happy said to the mouse.

"Well, you know I have a knack for getting the news," Roscoe admitted.

"Yeah, I know." Roscoe was the first to hear everything at Big Apple Barn. He always seemed to be in the right place at the right time. Then he would scurry around the stables, stopping at each stall to spread the word. "Sassy is really looking forward to this show," Happy continued.

"You're telling me," Roscoe replied. "She wouldn't stop yammering on about it. I'm glad you know about it. I think she was a little nervous to tell you, since you aren't going to go."

"Oh, I'm fine. I don't mind staying here," Happy explained.

"I'm with you. Who wants a ribbon hanging on his stall all the time? It seems silly to me."

Happy liked how Roscoe always said exactly what he was thinking. "You're right," Happy agreed. "It's just plain silly."

"I'm glad you're so easygoing, Happy," Roscoe said. "You're not at all like Dapper Dan."

Happy looked down at his friend. "Who's Dapper Dan?" he asked.

"Oh, that's the other news of the day," Roscoe explained, his eyes wide. "Dapper

Dan came home. He's the pony that lives in the big stall at the other end of the barn. He and his owner, Valerie, go to tons of shows. They've been away competing all summer, and he just got back."

Happy couldn't believe it. He had been at Big Apple Barn for more than three months, and the other pony had been away the whole time? No one had even mentioned his name.

"I would get homesick if I were gone that long," Happy said.

"Gosh, I would miss you," Roscoe told him. "I'm glad you aren't a show pony."

"That makes two of us," Happy declared. "Being a school pony is fine by me."

During Roscoe's visit the next day, Happy got his first look at Dapper Dan. The pony was walking down the aisle next to a girl with blond hair. Happy guessed that she was

Valerie, Dapper Dan's owner. As the pair passed his stall on the way to the indoor ring, Happy couldn't help but stare.

"So that's what a real show pony looks like," Happy whispered.

"Yeah," Roscoe said.

"He's so well-groomed," Happy noted. Dapper Dan's coat was shiny. The wide blaze on his face was a bright white, as were his four socks.

"He's *always* that neat," Roscoe replied.

Happy shook his own shaggy mane in disbelief. He thought Dapper Dan looked more like a statue than a pony, and his rider looked just as polished. Her golden hair was pulled back in a tight braid with a bow on the end.

With a brisk clip-clop, the pony and his rider headed to the indoor ring.

Happy and Roscoe looked at each other. Quickly, Happy lowered his head so Roscoe could climb on. Then they rushed to the back of the stall where there was a hole in the wall. The gap was big enough that they could look into the indoor ring and watch Dan and Valerie practice.

"They look good together," Happy said.

"They do," Roscoe responded from his seat between Happy's ears.

Happy had a feeling it took a lot of work to look that good. Were all show ponies as good as Dapper Dan?

Chapter Three

Fun and Games

The next day, Happy and Sassy took a break from playing tag in the field. Sassy had called time out for the second time. Happy knew she was tired of being it, but he couldn't help that. He was good at the game!

"Oh, look!" Sassy suddenly said with a gasp.

Happy had been busy rolling on the ground. There was an itchy place on his back, and rolling was the best way to scratch it. Besides, rolling was fun!

"Hurry!" Sassy insisted.

Happy scrambled to his feet and turned to see what Sassy was talking about. Near the fence, next to Diane, was Dapper Dan. Diane had opened the gate, and Dan was stepping into the field. Happy didn't understand why Sassy had gotten so excited. Dan was just a pony, and he was walking like any other pony would.

"He's coming this way," Sassy whispered. "What should I say?"

"Hmmm," Happy murmured, thinking. "I guess 'hello' would be a good start."

"Oh, right," Sassy replied. She swished her tail and lifted her head as the handsome chestnut pony approached.

"Hello," Dapper Dan greeted them. "I'm Dan. You must be the new school ponies. Roscoe told me about you."

"Hello," Sassy said. "Yes, we are the new school ponies. I'm Sassafras Surprise, and this is Happy Go Lucky, but you can just call us Sassy and Happy. And you're a show pony?"

"Yes, that is correct," Dan replied, but he didn't say anything else.

"That's nice," Sassy said.

Happy looked from Dan to Sassy. Sassy seemed uncomfortable, and she was talking in a funny way. She was saying every word very precisely. When Dan didn't respond, she said, "Maybe you can give me some pointers. My first show is this weekend."

"Are you going to Stillwater Farm?" Dan

asked. "It's just a small show, not like the ones at the fairgrounds. But I am going, too."

"I'm nervous. I hope I do well." Sassy watched Dan closely and waited for him to answer.

"Like I said, it's a small show. There won't be that many good ponies there. I'm used to bigger shows, but Valerie and I are going, anyway. We want to win a total of fifty blue ribbons this year."

"That sounds nice," Sassy said. Happy rolled his eyes a little.

"Yes," Dan replied. "We only need two more."

"Oh, wow!" Sassy gasped. She seemed to be impressed. "That's great."

Happy wasn't sure if it was great or not. Dan wasn't acting like a show-off, but he seemed to think he would win at Stillwater Farm, no matter what.

"Why, there's Big Ben," Dan said, looking across the field. "We used to go to shows together. I should say hello."

"We were just playing tag. You're welcome to join us after you've talked to Big Ben," Happy offered.

"Oh, yes!" Sassy exclaimed. "It's a great game. Happy's quite good. He can race around trees and make the tightest turns!"

Dan looked shocked. "You shouldn't do that," he advised. "You could hurt yourself."

"Oh, it's okay," Happy said quickly. "It's just for fun. You should play, too."

"Thanks, but I don't really have time," Dan said. "Valerie will be here to get me soon. We are going to practice our jumps today. Good luck, Sassy. Nice to meet you, Happy."

Sassy watched Dan walk away. "Wow, he's a real show pony," she said under her breath.

"He sure is," Happy agreed. Dan *was* a show pony, but that was really the only thing they knew about him.

Chapter Four

Practice Makes Perfect?

Later that week, Andrea and Ivy led their lesson ponies outside.

"We'll put Sassy and Happy in the small corral," Andrea told her little sister. "They can stretch their legs for a while. Then they'll be able to focus in our lessons later."

Happy was looking forward to his lesson with Ivy, but he wasn't looking forward to being left in the corral. The ground there was covered with dirt, not grass like the pasture. Plus, the corral was much smaller.

"Have fun, Sassy," Andrea instructed. "We need to practice for the show later." Ivy gave Happy a scratch behind the ears. Happy wished he could just go back in the barn with her.

As the sisters walked away, Sassy turned to Happy. "Well, you heard them. We have to stretch our legs. I want to work on my trot, so that my stride is nice and long."

Happy rolled his eyes. "Go ahead. I'll stay here," he said. He wasn't competing in the show, so what was the point of trotting laps? It was a hot day. He just wanted to stand there, put his head over the fence, and feel the breeze. *The small corral is boring,* Happy thought. *There isn't any grass to eat, and there isn't enough room for a really good run. We can't even play tag.*

But Happy didn't know if Sassy would play tag even if there was enough space. She had refused to play the day before because she didn't want to risk getting hurt. Now, out of the corner of his eye, Happy could see Sassy trotting from one end of the corral to the other. *Playing tag is much better than trotting laps,* he thought, taking a deep breath.

"A deep breath for a deep thought?" someone asked.

Happy searched around to find the owner of the voice. Sitting on the corral fence was a scruffy orange barn cat.

"Hello, Prudence," Happy said to his friend.

"Hello, Happy," the tabby cat replied. "I haven't seen you in the corral before." Prudence had been the barn cat long before Happy had arrived at the stables. She had been there when Happy's mom had been a school pony. She knew everything there was to know about Big Apple Barn. She was a good friend to ask for advice. She was always honest — sometimes too honest.

"We're supposed to be getting rid of our extra energy," Happy told her. "But I like my energy. I don't want to use it all up in here."

"I see," the cat replied. She gave her paw a slow lick.

As soon as Sassy noticed Prudence, she trotted over to the fence. "Prudence, you should tell Happy to trot with me," Sassy said.

"I'll do no such thing," Prudence replied. "He doesn't feel like running around in this heat, and I can't blame him."

"I bet Dapper Dan would practice his paces before a lesson," Sassy said.

"Well, I'm not Dapper Dan," Happy pointed out.

"That's for sure," Sassy agreed. "He's a show pony, and he has a huge championship ribbon on his stall door."

Happy couldn't argue with that. When Ivy

had led him to the corral that morning, Happy had seen Dan's ribbon. It was blue and gold and red, and it looked like a big satin flower. Even Happy thought it was beautiful.

"Dan may win ribbons, but that doesn't mean he is always right," Prudence commented wisely. "That pony isn't much older than the two of you, but he's been training for shows his whole life. That's about all he's done."

"Well, practicing seems like the most important thing to do if you are a show pony," Sassy said. "I wish Dan were here. He would trot with me."

"He might, but he might not," Prudence said. "Dan is a competitor. And since you will be competing against him, he might not see you as a true friend. Dan doesn't have many friends."

"Oh, I think he'd be friends with me," Sassy said.

"Winning is very important to him," Prudence said.

"And, did you notice," Happy added, "that Dan was sure he was going to win at Stillwater? He acted like he wouldn't even have to try to get those blue ribbons." As soon as he said those words, Happy was sorry. He could see Sassy tilt her head and squint her eyes as she thought things through.

Happy did not want Sassy to be angry with Dan. Dan wasn't mean. He didn't even brag all that much. He was just used to winning.

"You know, you're right. He doesn't think I have a chance!" Sassy exclaimed. "How dare he! Well, I'll prove him wrong."

Sassy whipped around and began trotting

again. Happy noticed that her stride was longer and faster than before. *That didn't work at all,* Happy thought. He had hoped Sassy would stop practicing. He wanted her to hang out with him by the fence, but now she was pushing herself harder than ever.

"This show business is messy stuff," Happy said to Prudence. The cat nodded slowly.

Just then, Ivy came running out of the barn. "Happy!" she yelled. "You'll never believe it!" Ivy climbed up the bottom rails of the fence, so her face was right next to Happy's head. "Mom said we can go to the show, too!" Ivy was so excited that she rubbed Happy's forehead too hard. "Isn't it great?" she asked, tickling Happy behind the ear.

Happy was glad he didn't have to answer her. Instead, he looked at Prudence and gulped.

Chapter Five

All Work, No Play

Happy was going to the show, whether he wanted to or not. It was clear that Ivy was excited. She would not stop talking about the show as she tacked Happy up for their lesson. Happy was surprised. Why did everyone think shows were so great? Why didn't he understand what all the fuss was about?

During the lesson, Diane explained what Ivy and Happy would do on the day of the show. They would get in the trailer very early in the morning, and drive to the show grounds. Then they would get a chance to practice before the show started.

The ponies and riders at the show were split into groups based on experience. Ivy was a beginning rider, so she and Happy would ride in the first group of show classes. Andrea and Val had been riding longer, so they were in the intermediate group. Their jumps would be higher, and their courses would be more difficult.

Happy was glad that he was in the easier group. It was a good place to start. And he was relieved that he wasn't competing against Sassy or Dan. They were both being so serious!

Except for the instructions about the show, Happy and Ivy's lesson was just like any other. They went through their gaits, practicing the walk, trot, and canter. Then they jumped some fences — not too high or too low.

"Terrific," Diane called. "Do it just like that at the show on Saturday, and you'll be bringing home some ribbons."

Ivy led Happy back into the barn, took off his saddle and bridle, and gave him a long pat. For a treat, she brought him back outside to a patch of grass. As Diane was raising the fences for the next class, Sassy, Andrea, Dan, and Valerie all walked into the ring.

"Good!" Diane said. "Since you are all showing together, I thought you could share a lesson."

"Fine by me," Andrea replied, shortening her reins.

Valerie just nodded her head and pulled herself up into the saddle. Happy thought it was odd that Valerie didn't say anything. As she rode Dan around the ring to warm up, she looked as serious as her pony!

At first, Happy was so busy eating that he didn't pay much attention to the lesson. But once Dan and Sassy started jumping, he forgot all about the grass.

"Wow! Look at Sassy go!" Ivy said. "Isn't she amazing?"

Happy tossed his head up and down. He

agreed. Sassy was jumping with more bounce than ever. Happy guessed she was trying to prove something to Dan. Dapper Dan might be classy with his four white socks, but Sassy had her own style. Her spotted back and the bright star on her forehead were flashy. If anyone had a chance of beating Dan, it was her.

"They both look so good," Ivy noted. "I'd hate to be that judge on Saturday. I wouldn't know how to choose the winner of the blue ribbon."

Happy thought Ivy was right. Both ponies looked incredible. He wished Sassy could think about something besides the show, but he still wanted her to win.

After the lesson, Andrea and Valerie walked their ponies together to cool them down. Happy wondered what Sassy was saying to Dan. Was she telling him that he would have to jump well to beat her, even though she was a new show pony? Happy hoped she was being nice.

The fact was, Happy liked Dan. He just didn't think they would ever be good friends. They didn't have enough in common.

"You know," Ivy whispered to Happy, "I like Valerie, but we're not really friends. She's away at shows most of the time. And when she's here, she never wants to go on trail rides or anything. She always has to practice. That's no fun."

Happy smiled at his rider. *I know just what you mean,* he thought.

Chapter Six

A Change of Plans

The next morning, Happy had a bad feeling when he woke up. It was Friday, the day before the show. Diane had told Ivy and Andrea they shouldn't practice anymore. Happy and Sassy needed to save their energy for the show. Instead, the sisters planned to take the ponies on a trail ride. Then, they'd give them a bath, so both ponies would be clean for the next day.

Happy was looking forward to spending the day with Sassy, especially since she wasn't allowed to practice. She'd have to have fun with him!

But when he saw Sassy walk down the aisle with Andrea, he knew something was wrong. Andrea put Sassy in the cross ties just outside of Happy's stall.

"Oh, no," Andrea moaned. "Oh, Sassy. Please, no."

Happy could see Andrea running her hands down Sassy's legs. "I have to get Mom," Andrea murmured. As Andrea ran out of the barn toward her house, Happy stuck his nose over his stall door.

"Sassy, what's wrong?" Happy asked.

"Andrea says my leg feels warm," Sassy said. "She thinks I'm hurt."

"Well, are you?" Happy questioned.

"I'm not sure," Sassy replied. Happy noticed that her eyes did not glow with their usual spark.

"How could you have hurt yourself? You wouldn't even play tag with me," Happy said.

"I know, I know," Sassy sighed.

"Listen, you can't be hurt," Happy reminded her. "We have a big day today. And the show is tomorrow!"

"Don't worry. It's probably not that bad," Sassy reassured him.

But it was. Diane came into the barn and felt Sassy's leg, just like Andrea had.  Next, she asked Sassy to trot. Happy could see that Sassy was limping. Diane shook her head and told Andrea that Sassy couldn't go to the show.

Sassy closed her eyes, and her head drooped down.

Happy knew that Sassy felt awful. He could not believe that she wasn't allowed to go to the show. And now he would have to go without her.

Getting ready for the show on his own wasn't any fun. Ivy decided not to go on a trail ride since Andrea and Sassy couldn't go. Happy had to have a bath on his own, too. Happy usually didn't mind getting all sudsy, but now it just made him nervous. All he could think about was what the next day would bring.

Of course, Ivy chatted with Happy as she washed him. "It's weird how Sassy started limping all of a sudden," Ivy said. "I wonder if she worked too hard yesterday. She did an awful lot of trotting in the corral before her lesson."

Happy didn't even want to think about it! Was she hurt because she practiced too much? Why couldn't she have just hung out by the fence with him?

"I know you must be sad," Ivy said. "It would have been nice for you and Sassy to go to your first show together."

Happy let out a deep sigh. He turned to look at Ivy. She was busy brushing pony shampoo through his tail.

"But if it makes you feel better," Ivy went on, "Andrea has another pony she can ride in the show. This pony is a real champion. She's won even more ribbons than Dan. She is going to meet us there."

What is Ivy trying to say? Happy wondered. That didn't make him feel better at all! He wanted Andrea to ride Sassy, not some other pony — especially not one who won all the time.

"Andrea is sad about Sassy," Ivy said, "but she's still excited to ride this other pony."

Happy blinked in disbelief. He had not wanted to go to the show in the first place. Now things seemed to be getting worse and worse.

Chapter Seven

The Big Hubbub

Roscoe climbed up the door of Happy's stall the next morning for an early visit.

"Wow, Roscoe, this is awfully early for you," Happy said. He knew the mouse usually napped until noon.

"What kind of friend would I be if I didn't come by to wish you luck?" Roscoe asked.

"Well, you *did* come by," Happy answered. "So I guess we'll never know."

Roscoe grinned. "Are you ready for the big show?"

"I'm not sure," Happy admitted. "I've never been to a show before. Remember? So I don't know what to expect."

"Oh, you'll be fine. You're gonna be with Ivy," Roscoe said in a kind voice.

"Yeah, but I wish Sassy were going, too. I want someone there that I can talk to," Happy explained.

"We can talk lots when you get back," Roscoe said. "You'll have to tell me everything. I bet you hear lots of great news." Roscoe paused. "And, you should know that I stopped by Sassy's stall. She's feeling a lot better. She said to wish you good luck."

"That's nice of her," Happy said.

"Yes," Roscoe agreed. "She is nice."

Roscoe stayed in Happy's stall until Ivy

came by with his leg wraps. Happy knew the wraps would keep him from hurting himself in the trailer.

"Thanks for keeping nice and clean, Happy. You look great," Ivy complimented him.

Happy had wanted to roll on the ground after his bath. His skin had felt dry and itchy, but he just scratched his back against the wall instead. It was nice of Ivy to notice that he had tried to stay clean. That was one thing Happy loved about Ivy. She could think like a pony.

When Ivy was done putting the wraps on Happy's legs, she led him to the front of the barn. Dan and Valerie were waiting by the trailer. Dan's mane was tied up in fancy braids. *Oh, so that's what Sassy was talking about,* thought Happy. He remembered his friend had wanted her mane in braids for the show. Happy liked his mane just the way it

44

was. Ivy had washed it well. No one would be able to tell that it was extra shiny if it was all tied up.

"So you're coming after all?" Dan asked.

"I guess so," Happy said. "But Ivy and I are in the beginners' class, so we won't be competing against you."

"Well, that's good," Dan replied. "It's always odd showing against friends."

Happy looked at Dan. *Are we friends?* he wondered. He couldn't even tell if Dan liked him.

"That's the good part about Sassy being hurt," Dan said.

Happy gasped. How could there be anything good about Sassy being hurt?

"It's awful that she can't come to the

show," Dan added quickly. "She's very nice. But she is also a strong jumper. It would have been hard to beat her. And I, of course, want to win."

Happy nodded as Dan was loaded into the trailer. Happy thought he understood what Dan was saying, even though he didn't agree with him. Dan knew that Sassy was a good pony. Dan liked her, but not as much as he liked to win.

After Ivy loaded Happy into the trailer, she gave him a kiss. "See you soon, boy," she said. She waved to him and ducked out the side door.

Happy swallowed as the door shut. He remembered the last time he had been in a trailer. It was when he had first come to Big Apple Barn. The ride was not very long, but he had been homesick for his mom and his old home before he arrived.

This ride was completely different. First of all, Happy wasn't alone. Dan was next to him. Second, they were headed to a show. It was a little scary, but not nearly as scary as moving to a new barn.

When the trailer door opened again, they were at Stillwater. It was still early, and the air was crisp and cool. Diane backed Happy down the ramp, and Happy breathed in the smells of the show. There were lots of ponies and horses there. There were the familiar scents of grass and grain. Maybe the show wouldn't be so bad after all.

"What do you think, Happy?" Ivy asked.

Happy was so busy smelling, listening, and looking around that he could not focus on Ivy.

"I'm going to get my pony for the day," Andrea announced as she walked away.

Happy narrowed his eyes. He wondered

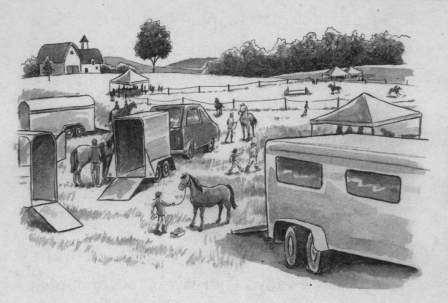

how Andrea could be so cheerful. After all, Sassy was still at home. But Happy did not have much time to think about Sassy.

"It's time to practice, Happy," Ivy said. "We need to hurry. We have to be done before they raise the jumps. They raise them so the more experienced ponies can practice, and they jump higher than we do." She ran the brush over his back and legs, then started to tack him up. "See how nice your saddle and bridle look, Happy? I cleaned them last night."

Happy turned to admire the saddle, but Ivy had already placed it on his back. The next thing Happy knew, Ivy pulled herself into the saddle and clicked her tongue. Happy walked down a dirt path. It led to a wide field that was roped off. Inside, there were all kinds of jumps. And all kinds of horses.

"This is our chance to see the ring and go over a couple of fences before the show starts," Ivy explained. Happy hardly heard her. He was busy taking it all in. Before Happy had moved to Big Apple Barn, he had lived in a small barn with just his mom. Until he arrived at this show, he had never seen so many horses in his life! Ivy nudged him with her heel, and he slowly walked into the ring.

Happy took careful steps. He did not want

to get in anyone's way, but it was impossible not to. There were just too many horses and ponies. Once, when Happy was trying to jump a fence, a stocky gray horse came straight at him from the other direction! "Watch out, pipsqueak!" the horse bellowed. "Move over, kid," another scolded. And it wasn't just the horses. The area outside the ring was a mess of trucks and trailers, and there were lots of dogs, too.

After they finished their practice time, Ivy rode Happy back toward Diane's pickup. His head was buzzing. There was too much to see and hear! Happy's eyes flashed all around.

"It's okay, boy," Ivy reassured him. She patted his neck, but just then a loud rattle filled the air. Happy stopped and raised his head, searching for the source of the noise.

"It's okay. That was just a trailer ramp coming down," Ivy explained. Happy looked around and saw that she was right. Happy knew that sound. He should not have been scared, but there was just so much going on. As they started off again, Happy did not understand why anyone would want to come to a show. He would rather stay home any day. If this small show was such a hubbub, what would a big show be like?

Happy really wanted to talk to someone. But Dan loved shows, and the pony Andrea was riding had won even more ribbons than Dan. She probably loved shows, too.

"You did a good job practicing, Happy," Ivy said. "Now we just have to wait here for our show classes to start."

Happy dreaded the competition, but he wanted to get it over with. Then they could go home.

"Hey, Happy," Ivy said as she jumped to the ground. "It looks like Andrea brought her pony over. Do you want to say hi?"

Happy gave a short snort. He wasn't in the mood for chitchat with the new pony just then.

"You don't seem very excited," Ivy noted. "Come on, you'll like her."

Happy sighed and didn't even look up.

"I'm sure you've met before," Ivy said. "Happy, this is Gracie."

Suddenly, Happy's ears pricked forward and his eyes brightened.

Mom?

Chapter Eight

Someone to Talk to

Happy could hardly believe it! When he had left his old stables, his mom had promised that they'd see each other again. Happy never imagined that it would be here at a show.

"Hello, Happy," Gracie said gently. She reached out and touched Happy's muzzle with her own, just like old times. "This is your first show, isn't it? Congratulations, son."

"Mom!" Happy gasped. "I'm so glad you're here!"

"I am, too. It's wonderful to see you," Gracie said. "You look good."

The excitement drained from Happy's face. Not even seeing his mom could make him feel better about the show. "I don't feel very good," Happy admitted.

"What's wrong, dear? Is everything okay at Big Apple Barn?" Happy's mom asked. "I was sure you would enjoy being a school pony."

Happy looked down at his hooves. "Oh, I do! It's this whole show thing. I'm not sure I like it."

"Ah," Gracie said. "I think I understand. There's a lot of hubbub, isn't there? A little too much going on?"

Happy nodded.

"And I suppose you're not quite sure how

54

you feel about competing against other ponies," Gracie added.

Happy nodded again, relieved that his mother knew him so well.

"I remember feeling just that way at my first show," Gracie said.

"Really?" Happy questioned. "But Ivy said that you've won lots of ribbons."

"Well, eventually. But I was all nerves at first," Gracie explained.

"Yeah, that's me," Happy said softly. "All nerves."

Just then, a voice crackled over the loudspeaker. "The first division of the day is for beginning riders. All beginning riders, ponies, and horses, please come to the ring."

"That's us, Happy," Ivy said.

"Okay," Diane said, rushing over "Let's take care of the finishing touches."

The next thing Happy knew, Diane was

combing his mane and tail. Andrea appeared out of nowhere. She squirted fly spray on a rag and smoothed it over Happy's coat. "See, we got off a lot of extra dust," she said, holding the dirty rag in front of Happy's face.

"Now it's time to do your hooves," Diane said. Before Happy realized what was going on, Diane had painted his hooves with a black gloss.

56

"You look like a real show pony now," Andrea said. He was so gussied up, Happy believed Andrea. But he still wasn't sure that he liked it.

Meanwhile, Ivy had also been getting ready. Her show hat was black velvet, and she wore a navy-blue jacket and black gloves with her tan riding pants.

"All set?" Diane asked.

"All set," Ivy answered. She put her foot in the stirrup and pulled herself into the saddle.

"You two look good together," Gracie told Happy. "I'll watch with Andrea from here. Don't worry, just have fun. That's the best advice I can give."

"Let's go!" Diane announced. She grabbed Happy's reins and led him to the show ring.

Lots of ponies and young riders were standing near the ring. There were some

57

horses, too. Happy thought everyone looked pretty nice, but no one was talking — no one except a gray pony and a dark brown horse standing closest to the gate. They were chatting loud enough for everyone to hear.

"I don't see many familiar faces around here," the horse said.

The pony shook his head. "No, this is a small show. The only other top pony I've seen is Dapper Dan. You know, he's trying for his fiftieth blue ribbon," the gray pony replied. "He has forty-eight already this year."

"Well," the horse said. "No one here will be able to beat him. That's for sure. He's just too good."

Happy found himself staring at the horse and pony. They both had their manes braided, and they acted like they knew what they were doing. Happy knew that they were probably only in the beginner group because of their riders. Happy guessed they went to shows as often as Dan. Suddenly, Happy felt out of place again.

"Okay, Happy," Ivy said, petting him on the neck. "Our number is 727. When they call it, we go in the ring."

That doesn't sound so bad, Happy thought. He watched as the gray pony's number was called.

"Up next is 724, Cloud Nine, ridden by Amber Levy," the announcer said. The gray pony trotted into the ring and made a small circle. Then he started to canter, and he cantered up over the first fence. There were four fences on the outside of the ring, and the horses had to go around the ring twice. When he was done, Cloud Nine trotted another small circle and walked through the gate. All the people watching clapped their hands.

He makes it look so easy, Happy thought.

Next was number 725, a small chestnut pony named Lucky Star. *This pony does not time his jumps as well,* Happy noted. *He takes a short step before all of the fences, so his takeoff isn't as smooth.* Happy didn't mean to be critical, but he did want to learn from the others' mistakes.

Number 726 was the big brown horse. Her name was Dazzle Me, yet Happy didn't think she was all that dazzling. Her timing was good, and she jumped well. But she looked bored. Happy remembered his mother's advice: *Have fun.*

The loudspeaker buzzed on, and Happy held his breath. "Number 727 is Happy Go Lucky, ridden by Ivy Marshall."

Ivy leaned forward in the saddle and scratched Happy behind the ear. "Come on, boy," she whispered. "It's our turn."

Happy closed his eyes and held his breath. *This is it.*

Chapter Nine

Showtime

Diane patted Happy's neck. "Okay, you two, go show them what you're made of," she said, smiling.

"Come on, Happy," Ivy said, nudging him with her leg as they entered the ring. At once, Happy put more spring in his step. They trotted in a warm-up circle. Now that it was their turn, Happy was having a hard time remembering just what to do. Luckily, he had Ivy there to help him. She clicked to

Happy, and he picked up a canter. He listened to Ivy as they headed toward the first fence. "Easy does it," she said in a hushed voice. Happy concentrated on keeping an even stride. As smooth as the velvet on Ivy's helmet, they were up and over the first fence and the next.

Ivy led him into the corner. The grass was deep there, and Happy had to really lift his legs as he made the turn toward the next two jumps. "That's it, Happy," Ivy whispered. "Isn't this fun?"

Happy thought about it. He realized he *was* having fun, just like his mom had said! The fences were fancy. The ring was big and grassy. And they had it all to themselves! As they approached a blue-and-white fence with yellow flowers on top, Happy pricked his ears forward. *Flowers on a fence?* he said to himself. *Now I've seen everything!* He wasn't sure he liked shows, but he did enjoy jumping a good course. He flew over the flowers with a mighty leap.

They went over the final five jumps with the same energy. After they were done, Ivy asked Happy to trot in a small circle. Everyone clapped as they left the ring. Happy liked hearing the  applause, and he liked it even more when Ivy reached around his neck to give him a big hug.

"You looked fantastic, Ivy!" Diane said, greeting them outside the fence. "And Happy, you're a real star."

"Do you think we'll win, Mom?" Ivy asked.

"You rode really well, honey," Diane said.

"I'd give you the blue ribbon, but it's up to the judge. She was watching how Happy jumped each fence. Did he lift his knees up high and keep them even? And did he keep a steady pace? She has a lot to consider." Diane ran her fingers through Happy's mane as she spoke. "But no matter where you place, you should know that you both did a great job. And you get to go two more times."

Ivy nodded that she understood. Happy did, too. They had three courses in all, so they had three chances to win a blue ribbon. But there were seven teams in the beginner group, so there was a lot of competition.

As they jumped their next two courses, Happy kept Diane's hints in mind. But Happy also remembered his mom's advice to have fun. He thought that was the most important thing of all.

Happy was so relieved when he finished his last show class that he started to walk back to Diane's truck right away.

"Whoa, Happy!" Ivy said, pulling on the reins. Happy stopped and turned his head, so he could see Ivy in the saddle. "We have to see if we won any ribbons before we can go home." Happy sighed and headed back toward the ring. He had been a good sport. He was having fun, but he was also getting a little tired. Showing was hard work!

"Don't worry, Happy," Ivy said, leaning forward in the saddle so he could hear. "I don't care where we place. I know we did great." But then the judge gave a paper to the announcer, and Happy saw Ivy cross her fingers.

The announcer walked over to the gate and picked up his bullhorn. "In the first beginner class of the day, first place goes to 724, Cloud Nine," the announcer said.

Of course, Happy thought. *Cloud Nine looked amazing. He deserves it.*

"And second place," the announcer continued, "goes to number 727, Happy Go Lucky."

"Congratulations, Ivy!" Diane rushed up and gave her daughter a hug. "You have to get your ribbon."

"Good job, Happy!" Ivy said with a pat. Happy could tell that she was excited. Then she clicked her tongue and steered him toward the gate.

"Nice work," the announcer said as he clipped the bright red ribbon on Happy's bridle.

After that, things were kind of a blur. Dazzle Me won the second class, and Happy got the red ribbon again. A black pony was

first in the last class, and Happy got another second place. Ivy gave Happy one hug after another. Diane couldn't stop smiling. She looked very proud. While Happy stood by the ring with Ivy, Dazzle Me and Cloud Nine came up with their riders.

"So you're Happy Go Lucky," Cloud Nine said. "Dapper Dan told us about you."

"You're having a good first show, aren't you?" Dazzle Me added.

"Oh, I don't know," Happy replied. "I'm just doing my best to have fun."

"Well, we're betting that you'll be going to the big shows soon," Dazzle Me said.

"I don't want to go to big shows," Happy explained.

"But you've got what it takes to be a real show pony. We'll see you there," Cloud Nine said. Before Happy could say anything else, the horse and pony walked away with their riders.

"Happy, guess what those girls just told me?" Ivy said. "They said we looked really good. They think we could go to big shows!"

Happy did not like the idea of being a show pony, but he *did* like to see Ivy smile. He wondered how happy she would be if they had won a blue ribbon.

Chapter Ten

A Pony Challenge

"Happy, you're the best, " Ivy said, leading him back to the trailer. She took off his bridle and gave him a carrot. "Let's get you untacked. Then we can go watch Dan and your mom in the intermediate division."

Happy loved that idea. He couldn't wait to see his mom jump. Ivy led him to a grassy hill near the show ring. He nibbled on clumps of grass and waited. When it was Gracie and Andrea's turn, Happy realized he was nervous for them. The intermediate courses were much more difficult, and the fences seemed very high. But Gracie and Andrea looked like they had practiced together all summer. Gracie snapped her knees up over every jump. She kept an even pace, and she looked like she was excited to be showing again. Happy was so impressed!

In the end, Gracie won one of the jumping classes and Dan won two.

"See, I told you she was good," Ivy said, rubbing Happy's forehead.

Happy nodded. His mom was very good. After seeing her, he couldn't wait to talk to her more about showing. Ivy walked Happy back to the trailer to wait for Gracie there.

As the ponies returned from the ring with their ribbons, Dan looked pleased. So did Gracie.

"It was an honor to show with you," Dan

said to Gracie. "I've heard so much about you, but you haven't been in a show for a long time, have you?"

"No, I haven't," said Gracie. "I've been busy doing other things." She looked at Happy and smiled. Happy knew what had kept her busy — taking care of him!

"Congratulations on winning your fiftieth blue ribbon, Dan," Happy said.

"Why, thank you, Happy," Dan replied. "I was so excited to meet your mom that I almost forgot."

As soon as Dan turned away, Happy started asking his mom questions. "How come you never said you were a show pony? How many ribbons did you win? How did Dan know about you?" Happy wanted answers!

"Oh, Happy," Gracie said, shaking her head. "I'm sorry I never told you about showing. It can be a big part of a pony's life. It was for me. Andrea and I competed quite often when I was young. We practiced hard, and we won a lot. That's how Dan knew my name." Gracie looked into her son's eyes. "But going to big shows takes plenty of work. I didn't want you to feel like you had to show, just because it's what I did. Many horses and ponies have more fun doing other things."

"Like playing tag?" Happy asked hopefully.

"Yes," Gracie said with a laugh. "Like playing tag."

Happy smiled at his mom.

"And some ponies like going to shows every once in a while, just not as much as Dapper Dan," Gracie added. "You can do whatever you want, son. But always remember to do what makes you happy."

For the rest of the afternoon, Happy enjoyed grazing next to his mom. They watched the later classes compete and chatted with Dan. Happy felt more comfortable with Gracie by his side. When Diane called to them, he had almost forgotten they were at a show.

"Ivy and Andrea, you have to get ready if you want to be in the Pony Challenge." Diane said. "You, too, Valerie."

"I don't know," Valerie replied. "Dan and I usually don't do that kind of thing."

"What is it?" Happy asked his mom.

"It's a class just for fun. You and your rider do an obstacle course, and whoever is the fastest wins. Andrea and I used to do that all the time." Gracie smiled. "It was my favorite part of the show."

Happy's eyes opened wide and he swished his tail. He couldn't wait!

Ivy stood up and brushed the grass off of her riding pants. "Happy and I are going to do it," she said. "You should, too, Val."

"I don't want Dan to get hurt," Valerie said.

"I think he'll be fine," Diane assured her.

Dan looked at Happy and Gracie. "Val and I have never done anything but the jumping classes," he explained. "But if you are both doing the Pony Challenge, I want to, too."

Dan suddenly turned to Val. He rubbed his face on her arm. Then he stamped his foot and threw his head up and down.

"Dan, stop it," Val said. The chestnut pony stomped his foot again. "What? Do you want do this Pony Challenge?"

Dan threw his head up and down.

Valerie gave her pony a funny look. "Well, okay. I guess we can give it a try."

The riders got their ponies ready and rushed over to the gate. On their way, they passed Cloud Nine and Dazzle Me standing next to a trailer.

"Hey, Dan! Where are you going?" Dazzle Me called.

"I'm going to do the last class!" Dan replied. "It's the Pony Challenge."

"Why would you want to be in that silly class?" Dazzle Me asked.

"Yeah, you're a real show pony," Cloud Nine chimed in. "You're better than that."

But Dan just kept going, right behind Gracie and Happy.

Chapter Eleven

True Blue

After all of the teams arrived for the Pony Challenge, the announcer explained the obstacle course. The rider had to walk into the ring, leading the pony. When the bell rang, the rider would climb on the pony's back. Then the pony had to run to a nearby barrel, and the rider would grab an apple from the top of the barrel. Next, they'd do a figure eight around two of the fences, then run to another barrel and grab a carrot off the top. Finally, they had to run to the finish line and drop the apple and carrot into a burlap sack.

"That doesn't sound too bad," Val said, after the announcer finished the explanation.

"But it can be hard to do it fast," Andrea replied.

Ivy didn't say anything. Happy wondered if she was thinking what he was thinking. Happy was thinking that this game seemed a lot like tag.

The riders all drew numbers to find out their order. Val and Dan were first. Andrea and Gracie would go second. Ivy and Happy drew number ten, which meant they were last. Then the announcer handed out little pouches for the riders to carry the apples and carrots in while they were riding.

Happy watched Val and Dan's turn. They were so polished that they looked like they were still in a show class! Val sat up straight, and Dan kept the same pace for the whole course. They did everything right, but it seemed like their time was slow.

Andrea and Gracie went next. The first half of their course was perfect. They were speedy and precise. But when they headed toward the carrot barrel, Gracie couldn't slow down to turn. They galloped right past the barrel and had to go back to get the carrot. They lost a lot of time.

Several other ponies and horses were in line to go before Ivy and Happy. Happy was getting anxious. But it was different from the way he felt before the beginning jumping classes. Now he was excited. He wanted to show everyone what he was made of.

At last, it was their turn. Ivy and Happy walked into the ring. When the bell rang, Ivy put her foot in the stirrup. As soon as

Happy felt her hit the saddle, he took off for the first barrel. He timed his turn just right. Ivy reached down and grabbed the last apple from the top of the barrel. Then Happy bolted toward the fences, making a tight figure eight between them before springing into a gallop.

As he ran toward the carrot barrel, Happy could feel Ivy leaning forward. He knew she was trying to keep her weight off his back, so he could go even faster. Happy made his stride longer and galloped to the second barrel. He slowed down just in time to make the turn — just like he did when he was playing tag around the apple trees at Big Apple Barn. As Happy circled the barrel, Ivy reached down and snatched up the carrot. They galloped down the stretch and skidded to a stop. Ivy tossed the apple and carrot into the burlap sack.

The announcer looked down at his stopwatch. "We have our winners!" he declared. "Ivy Marshall and Happy Go Lucky get the blue ribbon *and* the sack full of apples and carrots. Congratulations!"

Happy and Ivy were thrilled. Happy thought the Pony Challenge was much more fun to win than a jumping class.

"I must say, I am impressed," Dan said, as they all walked back to the trailer.

"You looked like you were having a wonderful time."

"I was!" Happy answered. "That was almost as good as a game of tag."

Dan gave Happy a long look. "And how did you say you win the game of tag?" Dan asked.

"No one really wins," Happy said. "You just play."

Dan tilted his head to the side, thinking. "You know," he said, "I believe I would like to play tag with you and Sassy sometime. If I am still invited."

"Of course you are!" Happy exclaimed. "That will be fun." He nodded to Dan, who nodded back, then walked away with Val.

Happy took a step toward his mom. Gracie reached out and touched his muzzle with her own.

"Happy, dear," she began. She swallowed and started again. "Happy, I'm very proud of you. You and Ivy are a good team. You could do very well at big shows if you decided to go." She paused and smiled. "But I know you'll do what is best for you, and that is what makes me happiest."

Happy reached out and touched his muzzle to his mother's once more. She knew him so well. He had enjoyed winning the ribbons, but nothing could beat seeing his mom again.

It was hard saying good-bye to his mom, but Happy knew he'd see her soon — maybe at a show. For now, he was headed back to Big Apple Barn.

As Ivy led Happy into the Big Apple Barn stables, she held his lead line in one hand

and their four ribbons in the other. So much had happened. Happy could not believe it was still the same day!

Happy whinnied good-bye to Dan as Val put him in his stall. Dan made him promise that they'd play tag the next day. Then Ivy clicked to Happy, and they headed down the aisle.

"Do you want to say hi to Sassy?" Ivy asked, stopping by the appaloosa's stall.

"Welcome back, Happy," Sassy greeted him. "Wow! Are all those ribbons yours?"

"Yep," Happy answered. "I got three for beginning jumping and one for a special class, the Pony Challenge. It was a race!"

"Gosh, Happy. I'm surprised. You sound like you had fun," Sassy said.

"I guess I did. You'd like it, Sassy. Maybe

85

we'll go when you feel better, and I'll show you the ropes."

"Thanks, Happy," Sassy said.

Just then, Roscoe and Prudence walked down the barn aisle and stopped at Happy's side. Ivy reached down to give them both a pat.

"I see you made it back alive," Prudence noted with a smirk.

"Yes, I did," Happy said. He knew his friend was making a joke. Happy had made it clear that he had not wanted to go to the show at all.

"And you brought home a ton of ribbons," Roscoe pointed out. "But I know you won't put them on your stall door to brag. That's silly."

Happy took a breath. He knew how Roscoe felt. He used to feel the same way, but going to the show had changed his mind a little. He decided to tell Roscoe the truth. "You know," Happy said, "I wouldn't mind if Ivy put up the blue ribbon. It was for a really fun class, and the ribbon proves that Ivy and I work well together."

Roscoe raised his eyebrows.

Happy held his breath.

"Well, if you put it that way," Roscoe said. "You *should* hang up that ribbon. Good job, Happy." Then Roscoe let out a little sigh. "Does this mean you'll go to shows every weekend from now on?"

"No," Happy answered with a shake of his head. "Shows are fun from time to time, but I want to do other things, too."

"I'm glad to hear that," Roscoe said. "Because Prudence and I would miss you."

Prudence looked from Roscoe to Happy and

shook her head. She wasn't about to admit that she'd miss him, but Happy knew she would.

"And *I* would miss *you*," Happy replied.

"Time to go back to your stall, Happy," Ivy said, continuing down the barn aisle.

"I have so much to tell you all tomorrow," Happy called over his shoulder to his friends.

"Congratulations on your first show!" Sassy, Roscoe, and Prudence said together.

As Ivy put Happy in his stall, he remembered talking with his mother that afternoon. He wasn't ready to be a real show pony, but he was glad he had gone to the Stillwater show. He watched Ivy hang their blue ribbon on his stall door. "You were wonderful today, Happy," she said, smiling. "But if it's okay with you, I don't want to go

to too many shows just now. Let's stay home and go on trail rides and play instead."

Happy nodded his head up and down. He couldn't agree more. And when he saw Ivy's smile, he felt like a real winner.

Glossary
Riding Clothes

Riding helmet —This can have a velvet cover, but the hard cap and a harness that fastens under the chin are important for safety.

Riding pants — *Jodhpurs* are long, stretchy pants worn with short paddock boots. *Breeches* are shorter than jodhpurs, and a rider wears them with high boots.

Riding shirt — The riding shirt has a high collar. It includes a choker, which covers the buttons and gives the outfit a formal look.

Jacket — Tailored jackets are usually worn in colors like navy blue, tan, or dark brown.

Boots — Younger riders can wear *paddock boots,* which are ankle high. Older riders wear *tall boots* that go up to their knees.

Gloves — These must be dark and thin, so the rider can feel the reins.